GASPERO

By

ELMA "APPLE" BRAUNSTEIN

Illustrations by the author

Print information available on the last page

Rev. date: 11/17/2015

To order additional copies of this book, contact:
Xlibris
1-888-795-4274
www.Xlibris.com
Orders@Xlibris.com

ACKNOWLEDGEMENTS

Brian Savage .....Whom I call my computer "guru" and had set up all the computer work.

Catherine Healy....Who has patiently edited "Gaspero" and has also written the introduction.

Thank you

G ive
A ll
S pecial
P eople
E qual
R ights
O pportunities

This book is intended to build tolerance in other children. Perhaps if children can see that special children can be heroes, I will have accomplished my goal.

Hopefully you will help me honor special needs children, their families and their friends.

Together we can raise awareness that will bring understanding and acceptance of all people.

Gaspero is an acronym that gives Gaspero his name.

My grandson is Hubie Clark who is Down's Syndrome. I am dedicating my book to Hubie, whom I love.

The white marble mausoleum sparkled as the early morning sun played with lights and shadows on its angled sides. The design of the building was made to look as if it were vaporizing into heaven while the white flowering trees and shrubs at the base softened the foundation line, making the total effect appear as if it was floating on a cloud. It's green spring grass lawn sprinkled with drops of opalescent dew slopes downward from the chapel to the town, and this added a consoling atmosphere to the cemetery.

Daybreak had arrived and the church bells from throughout the town began ringing, each with a different sound and a different rhythm. Some had sharp tones that seemed to sing a song and others had mellow tones that seemed to send waves of love.

It was the music of the morning. The bells continued ringing in sequence for about one hour, and the towns inhabitants were able to recognize the tones of their own church bell. The bellowing range of sounds brought feelings of all sorts to each individual – one could not escape the emotions, but everyone knew it was time to get out of bed and get going for the day! It was a signal to arise for work or church and somehow one felt obligated to do so as the neighbors could be watching.

****

The era was the 1930's. There were many newcomers arriving into our country from various nations around the world.

Gaspero was a mentally handicapped son of immigrant parents, from a Baltic country that decide to move to America. Inwardly or intuitively, his parents, not being able to express their real feelings publicly, hoped that help would be available for their only child.

Gaspero arrived among us being mentally handicapped at birth. Having never been coveted or cuddled, he was unaware of the feelings of a mother's warm soft breasts if she held him closely as a child. He was a living human whom was here or there but never embraced.

But we or he is never alone! Still, somehow he managed to grow up in a void. When there is a void from love in ones beginning, one does not miss what one never knew of, and Gaspero unknowingly, was never alone.

His three spirit guides that were assigned to him at birth had orders to protect and guide him through the lifetime on our planet, Earth.

No 1 Guide, who stands behind him, assists him in all his needs and protects him from dangers

No 2 Guide, who stands at his left, directs him to the sustenance's of life – such as food, housing, comforts, peace of mind etc.

No 3 Guide, Who stands at his right, oversees his creativeness, his awareness, his happiness of colors and flowers, his love of music and also the singing of the birds

What simple excitements can Gaspero be hiding inwardly after being born to be so very innocent?

Gaspero's guides were carefully leading him along his 'life's path' and at the same time, since we all have spirit guides, they were communicating with Elko's, Jenko's and Maya's by observing that the three were about to cave in from the stress! Immigrating was not out of the reach because an inheritance from an elderly aunt of Jenko's, gave them a bank account and a small house in a section of Queens, New York where most of those residing there were from the same area of the planet. They seem to have all arrived under similar circumstances: native clothes in cardboard suitcases, brogue shoes, head shawls and the women with scared and worried expressions. But for Jenko's and Elka, they had their own worrisome problem: Gaspero! How would this new world accept their son?

The inherited small row-house was like a palace to them compared to the mud floor cabin that they left behind.

The town of Queens was a polarized community of immigrants who were mostly factory workers, skilled repairmen, bakers, butchers etc. who filled the 'spaces' needed for the necessities of living a basic life style. These blue collar workers proceeded in making a living wage by persevering – they came to

America to acquire a better life and they were determined to succeed! Soon, as a whole, they became acclimated and they discovered the freedoms and opportunities available.

****

Elka and Jenko were the catapults to Gasperos life! Being completely unaware that the disappointment of their son really was a blessing to the Planet! (*He seemed to be guided blindly to a special path that led him to find simple needs for his sources of happiness.*)

The previous owners of their home had left a player piano and a cabinet full of player rolls.

Gaspero soon learned to sit on the piano stool and by holding on to the lip of the keyboard, he managed to reach the piano's pedals and by pumping them he could hear the musical tunes of the era :- "My Baby and Me", "Walking My Baby Back Home" etc.

From the onset, Maya, the buxom illiterate who was hired as a housekeeper and baby sitter and had been stealing cash and jewelry, was now becoming slovenly and mean. In fact everyone around him was growing old and feeble. His mother, feeling maternal guilt was drinking heavily and was going from one stupor to another. His father was becoming blind and senile.

Now it was up to them to place Gaspero out of harms way. Somehow the neighbors realized that things were abnormal and they went to the authorities whereas they took the only option available and placed Gaspero in an institution for Mentally Infirmed Boys.

At the Institution he shared space with other mentally handicapped young men that were placed there for various reasons and were in various stages of retardation.

In Gaspero's era, individual or mainstream education was unheard of and even though the community had no knowledge to lean in that direction, Gaspero innocently was about to make a contribution to other's lives. Since he came from a home where he was not coddled and he had to be as self-sufficient as he was capable of, he managed to be happy in his head by humming his favorite tunes.

****

Gaspero was now about fifteen years old and although he was mentally handicapped, he knew by the feelings that he was experiencing within his soul, that he was no longer part of his family or caretakers so he just walked out of the institution and never returned.

Being a teenager (this is a new word, not known in Gaspero's era) who never reacted with others of his own age. His emotions never showed disappointment, he was happy with his music, colors and just being free, to be himself. Did he ever feel lonesome? Was he ever feeling anger or was he born without a sense of violence? Was he free of emotions that left him open to be the ward of his guiding spirits? Were Gaspero and the three spirits all bound together and sent here to engulf a coming problem and save society?

Walking out of the Institution, although he was a sole figure, he was never alone – his three guides hovered over him and never left Gaspero, also he had many unseen friends that visited with him. *(We all have spirit guides that assist us on our daily paths.)* Gaspero's guides must be special as they are doing a great job of protecting him for whatever the assignment is that they were given.

****

It was a warm sunny spring day and the trees and gardens on his meandering route were bursting with color – red tulips, purple iris, yellow daffodils, white daisies etc. "Oh, these bright colors and blinding sunshine seemed to be there to make Gaspero happy." Did he know the colors by name? Did he know that the patch of lush grass was green and was waiting for him to lie down and rest as the evening was creeping in? Exhausted, he did lie down and fell fast asleep.

The chirping of birds, the milkman's truck, the trolley cars and the ringing of the bells awoke him as they did each morning. He felt rested and happy by being alone and in time he found other places to rest and sleep such as the graveyard and the city dump. In the city dump he found deserted shacks to cuddle up in especially when the weather was nasty. But he liked the cemetery, it was his flower garden! He did not understand the gravity of the place, only the beauty. The colors of the flowers and the scent in the breezes made him happy

Soon he discovered the Mausoleum. It was a very warm summer day and as he passed the doorway, he could feel the coolness escaping and it felt so nice on his body. Gaspero began gaining confidence and he liked visiting there. The attendant began noticing him and began to smile. Everyone in town now knew or knew of Gaspero. He never caused any problems, so when one day he appeared at the Mausoleum with an armful of apple blossom branches and he placed them in the bronze urn, the attendant was both surprised and pleased. He was surprised at the action and pleased with the display.

As a savant he had the ability and wisdom to be artistic with flowers. Savants are very special individuals. Usually they display one special talent such as playing a musical instrument, or painting, or drawing, or cooking etc.

Gaspero's eyes sparkled – he felt accepted! As time went on and he found his way, he felt joy in doing other pleasing things: Gaspero spoke with his eyes and as he silently went about town, he noticed that a newsboy was tossing the daily newspaper in front of each house. There were things that he was incapable of doing but he seemed to want to be needed. After observing that the people would emerge, walk down the path and bring the paper into the house, he suddenly followed rote and did it for them by carrying the papers to the front door.

Sometimes, having a certain gift, it becomes an instrument of capability and duty. So with a wide grin and those sparkling blue eyes, each morning Gaspero, half skipping and half running, would enter the cemetery and go directly to the bronze doors carrying his bundle of blossoms, leaves, twigs or tall grasses. *(This deep inane excitement must have had to evolve from another lifetime as there was no clue to such beauty and peace that was being absorbed from this lifetime on this plane in this era.)*

Gaspero made an existence for himself with the assistance from his spirit guides because of his pleasant demeanor which made him known and liked.

One can only imagine what any of his past lives could have been:- Perhaps he was a gardener to a royal family, or a jester, or a conqueror or even a King or a Queen as one can spend a lifetime being of either gender. Whatever he was, he is content at this time to be at peace with himself.

On this lovely spring day, and as usual, Gaspero is preparing to enter the Mausoleum and in fact he seems anxious as he awaits the click that responds to the unlocking of the great bronze doors.

As the cool air escapes along with the scent of the flowers, he hops and skips with happiness in his smile as he enters heading straight toward the large urn to place his bouquet of blossoms.

Today seemed as normal as every other day as he performed his daily routine except on that this day he never noticed a foul smell! A GREENISH BLACK SLIME WAS OOZING OUT OF A TOP LEVEL CRYPT! It was hissing and gurgling and foaming as it crept down the wall to the floor where it puddled near the entrance. The thick gooey slippery slime had a most repulsive, stomach revolting odor – it was the smell of rotting death! Gaspero never noticed even though the acrid smell made his eyes tear as he trod through, his footing slipped, and he still did not pay attention.

****

Gaspero was his happy self as usual as he slopped through the slime with his worn split-open shoes that he found in the local dump. Perhaps he did not have a sense of smell but he did have a sense of duty. He had an inner compulsion to perform his self imposed sense of duty.

The slime stuck to his big toe making it feel very hot as if it was on fire. He hurriedly fixed the flowers and let out a moan as he wiped his toe with his bare hands – now his hands began to feel creepy!

Not knowing what to do he began to walk and run at the same time towards his shanty in the town's dump. But still, on his way, he saw the rolled up newspapers and dutifully he picked up each paper and placed it on the porch or at the doorway of each house. EACH PAPER WAS NOW CONTAMINATED WITH THE SLIME!

****

The sky was darkening and it did not occur to him that he had a problem, still Gaspero was shocked with fear! This never happened to him before! Had he ever called anyone for help? As he was stumbling around he saw a patch of lush green grass that he plopped down on and with tears running down his cheeks, he fell fast asleep. Exhaustion and fear made Gaspero collapse on the spot!

No one knows how lonesome he felt or how long he laid there, but it was the excruciating pain in his hands and foot that awoke him. Also, as dawn was breaking the fierce burning pain and fear were still with him. Poor suffering Gaspero looked at his hands, he then managed to look at his foot – his skin was moving in all directions!

The sky was getting lighter and fright was over taking him. Gaspero had felt the pain of being burned before when he touched a red hot cinder but now he could not run away from this terror that be felled him.

The sunrise brought an even scarier sight. Now he could see where his hands and the exposed part of his foot were moving and wiggling in all directions. Gaspero, with eyes bulging, was looking at a very weird sight – on his hands and on his foot were things that he never saw before. Automatically, he tried to brush them off. The sight of the GREEN WORMS WITH YELLOW HEADS AND THREE RED ROLLING EYES was too much for this very brave soul to understand. Gaspero yelled, screamed and moaned and then collapsed! Gaspero fell backwards hitting his head on a rock! He laid there with no movement.

Laying there and unaware of being 'out-cold' from his fall, the worms were squirming with their mouths wide open – they wanted more slime to eat!

At the same time the birds were waking up. The robins, crows, starlings, blue jays, sparrows etc. began diving towards his hands and foot. Scared and confused, Gaspero began rubbing his eyes and ears and now the worms were growing out of his eyeballs, his eyelids and his earlobes! HE WAS A FEAST WAITING TO BE DEVOURED! He was so very frightened by this sight that he never arose. The birds began fighting each other as they dove trying to steal the bounty from each other. Some of the birds flew back to their perches acting kind of drunk from their fill and others flew about town.

Soon their feces were dropping in playgrounds, and in back yards. and children were bringing home the 'seeds.' Mothers were stroking the sore areas trying to relieve the pain .The sore areas were afflicting everyone and that really caused havoc in the city. Those whom handled the newspapers had worms growing out of their fingers, scalps, tongues and everywhere they unknowingly spread the slimy black residue on themselves and others. Parents would not hug their children or each other as they began to realize the cause of this pestilence. Those with the worms growing attached to their eyeballs were blinded and were unable to leave their homes, and others whom were able to emerge, suddenly found themselves blinded and could not find a way home. The streets were in total chaos as people were bumping into each other, falling and screaming in pain.

Cities and hamlets were in a panic as the pestilence was spreading as fast as a lightning bolt. Now the villages are contaminated and in the outskirts cows, pigs, goats etc. and the farmers, were being consumed by the plague! Everyone was stricken and very scared!

****

Gaspero began rolling in the grass over and over, to get some relief from the gnawing pain. Jolting, he got up from the grassy slope and began running. He ran and ran and was heading towards the town quarry. The quarry was one his favorite places where he found solitude. *(An unseen power seemed to be guiding him in that direction.)* With arms waving and tears rolling from his blinded eyes, he arrived there and avidly continued running toward a grey mountain of stones. He began climbing and with each step the stones began rumbling down its side. As the grey stones were tumbling down, one could see tiny sparks from the flint stones that were striking other stones. Gaspero persevered at working his way to the top to reach for that something bright that was there. The loosening stones were causing a rockslide. The sound was deafening as the mountain of stones seemed to be evaporating before ones eyes! Gaspero was still hanging on to its side and still continued climbing as if he had wings. Surely he had help from spirit guides that directed him to go to the quarry, after all, he was blinded, no one ever heard him speak and he seemed to be cared for and protected from daily crises. He managed to survive and still carry his broad smile to the universe and at this moment he was determined to grab whatever that bright thing was at the top of the pile of rocks "that was calling to him."

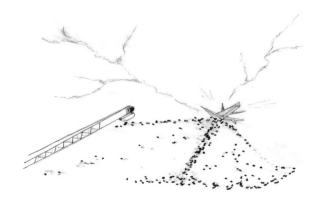

Gaspero visited the quarry often. It was a happy place for him where he could find many stones of many different colors such as crystals or quartz that were white, blue, lavender or pink and where there were also chunks of marble that seemed to sparkle in the sunlight. This time he was climbing the rock pile with a fierce determination to reach the top! He loved color and sparkling things, perhaps it was his innocence that never stopped him from reaching for them or was he living his preplanned path that was assigned to him at birth? Certainly his unseen guides were watching over him.

He scrambled with each step while trying to grab rocks with his hand, and yet with each attempt his foot would slip as the rocks would continue to crumble on that side of the mound. Finally he reached the top and he was able to grasp the large piece of crystal quartz prisms that were pulsating in the moonlight! It was shaped like an exploding star! Gaspero grabbed it, holding it close to his bosom! The pulsations, lighting up his face, showed that he was still in great pain and one could also see that he was laughing and sobbing at the same time while he was screaming, "Mama, Mama!"

Somehow it seemed that he knew something that no one else was privvy to. He seemed to be guided to the quarry! He was guided to the star rock! Was he aware that it was to create a miracle?

Gaspero had to be more spiritually guided then his peers. The spirits that were assigned to him at birth and were with him at all times to protect and assist him, were they also guiding him to use his abilities that he was not aware of? Perhaps, like calling "MAMA, MAMA" for the first time? The spirit guides were given this assignment to take their ward through this scourge in order to save mankind and the planet:- Thus making Gaspero the only living soul capable of doing this 'job' correctly

****

It was now daybreak and the sky instead of becoming brighter, was becoming darker and darker. Suddenly a piercing bright ball of light careened across the sky heading towards Earth as if being absorbed by the "Happy Rock!"

Our Planet Earth began to tremble and crack open spurting fluorescent liquids that gushed into the waters.

The meteorite was neon blue and neon green. It had a fluorescent pink tail that was spinning and whirling like an imaginary sea monster! As it entered into our gravity zone traveling in an orbit around our planet, all the streams, rivers, lakes and oceans turned fluorescent blue, green, yellow, purple, pink and orange! The sight was magnificent, that is if anyone could open their eyes to see it.

The Earth began to quivver, it began to rain and the sky bellowed with lightning belching ear cracking thunder! The torrents of rain were in Technicolor making the scene alarming and spectacular! No one ever experienced these happenings before – a phenomenon was occurring, the planet was shaking off its dirtiness and pollution!

As people looked at each other, the worms were turning black, shrinking and falling off of the bodies. Everyone was opening their mouths to drink the rainwater. They could now open their eyes to see the entire vista and to find that it turned into every color of the spectrum. Everything in sight seemed fresh and new and healthy! Planet Earth survived a cleansing! Even the fish in the sea glowed! The waterfalls and streams shown like diamond dust! There was also a glowing orange sunset!

****

Gaspero began sliding downwards on the mountain of stones while trying to grasp a hold with one hand and hold on to the Happy Rock with the other, still the stones kept tumbling down as they carried him along. Gaspero and the Happy Rock landed on the ground with a thud and a moan! Gaspero was lying there on his back. HE WAS NOT MOVING! His two hands were tightly holding the pulsating crystal "Star" to his chest!

No one knew how long Gaspero was lying there but someone heard dogs barking and yapping and decided to go and investigate. It was discovered that three black dogs surrounded Gaspero and a white dog with black and tan markings was licking his face. (*Perhaps these dogs must have known by the vibrations emanating from Gaspero that they had reason to awake him. Was it really animal instinct to awaken him from his comatose condition, or did they know something more than humans whom the real hero was? Do animal guides speak to human guides?*) He was certainly being cared for by unseen friends. Slowly, slowly, Gaspero opened his eyes. Now the dogs were cuddled close to his body as if to keep him warm.

It is now early morning before dawn and Gaspero is still holding the "Happy Rock" close to his chest when he began smiling! Above him was a magnificent rainbow whose colors were vibrant against a lapis blue sky. This happening excited Gaspero and he began to sit up and check out his surroundings.

WOW! The ground had patches of yellow, orange, green, blue, red and purple – all the colors of the rainbow. Gaspero jumped to his feet and began skipping and running from one color to another. If he was in a purple patch, he was purple. If he was in a green patch, he was green. I f he was in a red patch, he was red and if he was in an orange patch he was orange. His favorite color was yellow. As he was skipping and jumping and laughing in the yellow patch, and joyfully waving his pulsating "Happy Rock" in the air, a sudden flash of lightning struck down on him. The thunder, the loud cracking sounds and the 360 degree kinetic lightning bouncing off the hillsides was very scary! A second blast cracked directly above Gesparo taking his last breadth away and then

GASPERO BECAME SOLIDIFIED!

The community's population came running from all directions toward the glowing prisms. His gentleness and his euphoric demeanor left everyone remembering the compassionate wisdom that he carried with him. Now knowing Gaspero and his warm colored and glowing aura, we realize that he has given us a wider vision to assess all those that do walk among us.

GASPERO IS NOW A GOLDEN STATUE!

The statue is mounted on a base of sparkling quarry stones. Gaspero's image is of a happy, smiling, arm waving, jumping on one foot statue with the pulsating "Happy Rock" held high and lighted forever for all who loved and were enlightened by him. Also, for remembering as being peaceful, non violent, handicapped and brave!

At the base surrounding the statue and accompanying him forever. Are the silver statues of four dogs encircling the mound of stones, lying low enough so that each can easily be petted by all visiting children – especially those that are handicapped.

THE END

Gaspero has been called back now that he has fulfilled his chores in this lifetime. We have all had many previous lifetimes. We are here to learn lessons.

Printed in the United States
By Bookmasters